CRIMINAL CHRISTMAS VOLUME 2

CONNOR WHITELEY

No part of this book may be reproduced in any form or by any electronic or mechanical means. Including information storage, and retrieval systems, without written permission from the author except for the use of brief quotations in a book review.

This book is NOT legal, professional, medical, financial or any type of official advice.

Any questions about the book, rights licensing, or to contact the author, please email connorwhiteley@connorwhiteley.net

Copyright © 2023 CONNOR WHITELEY

All rights reserved.

DEDICATION
Thank you to all my readers without you I couldn't do what I love.

AUTHOR OF THE ENGLISH BETTIE PRIVATE EYE SERIES

CONNOR WHITELEY

CHEATER AT DINNER

CHEATER AT DINNER

Surrounded by rows upon rows of stunning white tables with their perfectly pressed napkins, posh cutlery and people sitting there dressed in stunning suits and dresses, Bettie English, private eye, turned her head and focused on her table.

As she breathed in the amazing smells of rich meats, expensive fruity wine and freshly steamed vegetables, Bettie couldn't help but smile as she stared at the most amazing plate of food she had ever seen.

She loved how the traditional British Christmas dinner looked like an expensive painting on the plate with its golden crispy roast potatoes, stunningly sliced juicy pork and Bettie's favourite the succulent, vibrant colours of the vegetables on the side.

Bettie could almost taste how crispy and vibrant the vegetables' flavours would be from here, their amazing sweetness would be sheer perfection against the juiciness and meaty flavours of the pork.

The sound of people talking, chatting and laughing all around Bettie made her force her attention away from the amazing, stunning food and on the equally beautiful person she was with.

As she looked up from the plate (longing to taste the delicious dinner), she saw her cop boyfriend Graham smiling at her as he poured a fruity red wine into her glass.

A part of her wondered if she should get him to stop, but she was here as a private eye and a girlfriend, so she might well blend in.

Watching her beautiful boyfriend with his perfect hair, jawline and body, Bettie took a few shallow breaths of the amazingly scented air as she knew this was going to be a perfect evening. She had a delicious dinner (that she really wanted to eat) and the love of her life, which she hadn't seen for a few weeks.

When Graham put the wine bottle down, they both just stared at each other for a few seconds and Bettie loved that. She knew it probably looked weird to other people but she loved all the time she spent with (and admiring) Graham.

The sound of cheering filled the restaurant so Bettie turned, smiled and her eyes narrowed as she looked at a couple who were hugging and kissing and everyone was clapping around them.

She knew they had just gotten engagement and a part of Bettie admired the man was being so ballsy and proposing in public. Bettie was still getting used to the whole relationship thing with Graham, but she loved him and he her.

Marriage might have been a long time away, but Bettie wanted it one day, one day far from now.

Then Bettie saw Graham cross his arms and smiled.

"So why ya wanna come here?" Graham asked.

Bettie gave him a massive smile. "What do you mean? Can't a girl take her man out on the town?"

"A girl or woman can. You don't,"

Bettie pretended to be offended and they both laughed.

That sole reason was why Bettie loved him and she would give anything to always see that amazing smile of his.

But he did have a point she supposed, they were always working, busying and helping others so much that they often forgot to work on each other, in more ways than one.

And tonight was no different.

"Look my left and tell me what you see," Bettie said.

She watched Graham carefully as he subtly turned his head and his eyes narrowed on a table.

"What the two dudes in the business suits?" Graham asked.

Bettie looked left and shook her head. "No,"

As she subtly pointed with her eyes at another table, and when Graham smiled she knew he had seen what they were looking for.

Mr Nero Alessandria was apparently some hotshot new businessman in London but Bettie had seen some of his speeches and companies, she wasn't that impressed but given that his wife had paid her a few thousand pounds to follow him, Bettie didn't really care.

It was even better that the wife had done almost all of Bettie's hard work by giving her all his contacts with pictures, addresses and phone numbers.

Bettie bit her lip a little when she remembered some of the rumours she had found online about him, apparently he was a ruthless man capable of horrible things but she hadn't seen any proof of that.

It still worried her though.

And when Bettie had found possible evidence of an affair with Mr Alessandria and the mystery woman meeting at a fancy London restaurant tonight, Bettie knew she wasn't going to refuse. Especially when her terms of employment always being the client pays for all needed costs. A fancy meal or two for getting evidence sounded like a needed cost.

Granted Bettie knew she would have to have a more compelling reason when she sent the invoice to the client.

The amazing smell of those beautifully golden, crispy roast potatoes made Bettie return her attention to the utterly stunning dinner in front of her. Bettie wasn't sure how much longer she could contain herself with that perfectly sliced juicy pork just staring at her.

"I presume ya hear for photos?" Graham asked.

Bettie nodded and subtly turn her head to focus more on the person sitting opposite him.

From where she was Bettie couldn't see too much about the woman, but it was definitely a woman. Bettie noted the woman's long blond hair, slim body and large assets. But she couldn't remember seeing anyone who matched the description in the information the wife had sent over.

"What ya waiting for then? Take some pictures?" Graham asked.

Bettie smiled, shook her head and rubbed his warm hands.

"I can't just take photos. Right now it is just a man and a woman sitting together. A lawyer would simply say it's a friend, a missing daughter or even his good looking mother,"

Graham's eyebrows rose at the last two.

"I'm not kidding," Bettie said.

Releasing Graham's hands wonderfully warm hands, Bettie picked up her posh knife and fork and sliced into the pork.

Just the ease of which the pork was cut got Bettie excited, her pork was normally rough and tough, but this... this was something else.

When she popped the pork into her mouth, she thought she was going to faint at how amazing it was. The succulent juices with their rich meaty flavours flooded her senses and the meat dissolved in her mouth.

This was going to be a night to remember.

As Bettie continued to eat the best dinner she had ever had with those golden crispy potatoes being her true favourites, she constantly flicked her eyes over to Mr Alessandria and the mystery woman.

The more Bettie focused on them, the more she couldn't understand what was going on. Even her and Graham who were working but still a loving couple, they were laughing, smiling and talking whenever they weren't eating.

But Mr Alessandria and the mystery woman weren't.

Bettie couldn't understand how they were looking at each other and barely speaking. It was almost like they weren't on a date but something else was going on.

After a while of subtly looking at them, Bettie put down her cutlery, finished off her amazing golden crispy potato and looked at Graham.

"You aren't a cop tonight are you?" Bettie asked.

Graham's eyebrows rose. "No. Why would ya ask

that?"

Bettie smiled, took out her phone and dialled a number.

"Cos I'm doing something questionable,"

"Who ya calling?"

Bettie smiled at the thought of hearing her wonderful nephew Sean who should still have been at her office with his boyfriend. She had said to him just to do her filing but Bettie knew he would have done other stuff too, which was why she hadn't cleaned her office in the past week.

"Calling Sean,"

"He and Harry wouldn't be in the office?"

Bettie smiled and just looked at him. "Two young boys alone in an office together. Away from my sister and her husband. They aren't going to be there. Seriously?"

Graham nodded and went back to eating.

Sean answered sounding a bit out of breath. "Hi Aunty,"

"Sean I'm going to send you a picture and I need you to try and find out who it is. Check the information the wife gave us first. I might have missed something,"

"Okay,"

"Thank you," Bettie said as she hung up, took a picture and send it to him.

When she turned back to Graham he had his normally ruggedly handsome cop face on.

"How you goanna identify it?"

Bettie rubbed his hand gently. "It's perfectly legal. I always save the questionable software from the dark web as a last resort,"

Graham gave her a sort of nervous chuckle and

he went back to eating his dinner. Bettie felt her body relax and tense and relax again as she realise she had just basically lied to him. As much as Bettie loved that dark web software from time to time, she knew it was 100% illegal.

But worth every penny.

Pushing those illegal thoughts away, Bettie picked up her cold glass of wine, breathed in the fruity hints and pretended to slip it.

When her eyes flicked back over to Mr Alessandria, Bettie put the wine glass down and her eyes narrowed. He was waving his finger at the woman like an angry parent would at a child.

He was clearly mad and probably struggling to keep his voice down.

Bettie wondered what he was talking about, he was a business owner so maybe it was something to do with that, but then Bettie remembered all the financial records and everything looked okay. Mr Alessandria had plenty of new investors too so he was set financially.

She had to get more information.

"Graham," Bettie said her eyes moving back to him. "Want to do a bit of acting?"

Graham frowned and Bettie smiled.

"I was wondering why I was here," Graham asked.

"Oh darling you're here because I love you. And Sean's too young to play certain roles and her sister would kill me for getting him involved too much in the Private Eye world,"

Graham shook his head. "Fine, what do you want me to do?"

"Easy. We get into a fight. I storm off towards

the target. We both take a glass of wine. We spill over them,"

"Then they go to the loos and follow 'em,"

"Exactly,"

Graham filled up the wine glasses again and giggled like a little schoolboy.

"Please Graham. Act serious," Bettie said laughing herself.

Both of them took a deep breath, made sure no one was watching and blow each other a kiss.

"You what! You sold my car!" Graham shouted.

Bettie was a bit taken back. "Well. You're useless. Lazy! I work all day and you do nothing!"

People were starting to look.

"You didn't have to sell my-"

"It isn't your car Graham. I paid for it,"

"It's our money. We're married,"

"Maybe we shouldn't be. Your mother is a such a nob too!" Bettie said.

Everyone was watching now.

Bettie shot up and grabbed the wine glass.

"Don't ya dare talk about my mother!"

"She's horrible. She hates me!" Bettie said.

She started to storm off.

"She's right Bet. I hate you too. You are so controlling!"

Bettie glided through the rows of tables.

She was almost at the target table.

Mr Alessandria stared at her and Graham.

"I wouldn't have to be so controlling. If you were useful. You gold digger!"

Graham grabbed her.

Bettie turned around.

"That's right Graham. You're a gold digger. A

dickhead. I'm leaving you!" Bettie shouted.

Throwing her wine glass.

The wine covered Mr Alessandria.

"Fine then nob!" Graham said throwing his wine over the other woman.

"You idiots!" Mr Alessandria shouted.

Bettie and Graham turned around and their hands covered their faces.

"Oh my god. I am so sorry sir," Bettie said, grabbing a napkin off a table and helping him clean it up.

Graham did the same for the woman.

"Go away. I need to clean up," Mr Alessandria said as he stood up, marched off and went into the toilets.

Bettie nodded at Graham and he left.

As she watched him go into the toilets, Bettie stared at the tall slim woman at the table and saw her just stare into space, she didn't even bother trying to clean herself up.

It was about this time Bettie realised that she hadn't needed to get wine over the mystery woman, but there was something off about her.

Sitting down on the horribly warm chair, Bettie looked at the woman and waited for her to ask why Bettie was sitting there, or how was she after the fight.

But the woman just stared.

Feeling her phone vibrate in her pocket, Bettie took it out and smiled when she saw it was a message from Sean telling her the woman was actually a new investor called Lady Penelope Bishop, some rich daughter of the English nobility.

"You don't look like a Penelope," Bettie said.

Penelope looked up at her.

"What were you two arguing about?" Bettie asked.

Bettie wondered if the woman was going to leave when her eyes kept switching between the door and Bettie, but after a few seconds Penelope stared into Bettie's eyes.

A part of Bettie felt as if Penelope was borrowing down into her soul, yet Bettie was surprised that this clearly fierce capable woman would allow Mr Alessandria to moan at her.

"Are you police?" she asked.

Bettie shook her head. "No but that is all you need to know,"

Penelope stood up. "Then whoever you are, I do not need to speak to the likes of you,"

"One scream from me and a police officer runs out of that bathroom," Bettie said coldly.

Penelope stared at her.

"I will scream. You know the lengths I go for my acting," Bettie gestured to the red wine stains on Penelope's dress.

"Fine. I am investing millions of your pounds into his company for a favour,"

Bettie's eyes narrowed, she wasn't from here and the way she said *your pounds* wasn't right, it sounded evil, dark and mysterious all at the same time.

Then the more Bettie looked at the woman, the more she realised that the woman definitely wasn't British and probably had ties to overseas crime.

"Who are you?" Bettie asked.

"I am just a businesswoman the same as you. But unlike you I presume you own your pockets. I do not. I have all the money in other pockets that I can play with,"

Bettie partly wanted to explain how her client was paying for all of this tonight, but this didn't seem like the real moment for accuracy.

"What is this favour?"

Penelope smiled and stood up. "Miss whoever you are, I urge you to go back to your table and finish. Tell your client…"

Bettie stepped forward. "How many Private Eyes have come for you?"

Penelope placed a gentle hand on Bettie's shoulder.

"So, so many. But you should know that your London is filled with opportunities and criminal gangs. So many wonderful opportunities for me and my kin to spread, work and love,"

Bettie felt a shot of icy coldness wash down her spine as she watched Penelope gather up her things and prepare to leave.

"What do I tell my client?"

"That man rejected us tonight. Don't do everything. She'll be rich soon enough,"

Bettie smiled and felt her stomach churn and tighten.

"Don't come for her," Bettie said bitterly.

Penelope stopped and stared Bettie dead in the eye. Again Bettie felt as she was having her soul burrowed into.

"You have yourself a deal. But I will call on you one day. I will find out who you are and you will do a single case for me,"

Bettie stopped and wondered if this was the only way to keep everyone safe, it didn't sound unreasonable. Her client would soon be rich but…

Bettie hated the feeling of sitting back whilst something terrible happened.

Bettie knew this woman spoke perfect English, but there was more to it, a much darker side that a part of Bettie didn't want to get involved in. She wanted to tell Graham about it, but this was out of his jurisdiction and she remembered what these gangs were like.

She had to protect Graham.

"Fine. One case. Don't come to my client for help," Bettie said then realised something. "How did you know my client was the wife?"

Penelope started to walk away but she said a final message to Bettie in perfect Russian. "We always watch,"

As Bettie stared at Penelope (or whoever she really was) walk out of the restaurant, she felt her entire stomach tighten into a knot and even the amazing smells of the perfectly sliced, juicy pork couldn't relax her.

The sound of Graham and Mr Alessandria walking up behind her made Bettie tense even more as she knew she couldn't warn Mr Alessandria in front of Graham. As much as Bettie loved him, she knew he was far too good of a cop and the last thing she wanted was him investigating the Russians.

And something deep, deep inside her knew everything would be okay in the end. The client would be rich, the questionable businessman dead and Bettie only had to do one case for a potentially dangerous Russian woman.

Bettie smiled at the craziness of it all so she shook Mr Alessandria's hand, bid him good night and walked back over to her table.

As she sat down, Bettie stared at what was left of the golden crispy potatoes, perfectly sliced juicy pork and the most amazing vibrant vegetables she had ever seen.

Picking up her cutlery, Bettie knew the food would be cold but it would still be amazing and worth every single bite.

At the sound of Graham pouring them another glass of the rich fruity wine, Bettie stared wide eyed at him as she admired his beautiful hair, face and body.

"Merry Christmas Bet,"

Bettie gave him a schoolgirl smile. "Merry Christmas Graham,"

CRIMINAL CHRISTMAS VOLUME 2

SALVATION IN THE MAID
13th December 1942
Northern France, Europe

Janet Berin might have just been a so-called simple country woman who served as a maid to a wealthy estate owner in Northern France but she wasn't always like that. As a child she had dreamed of grand adventures in Paris, Marseille and she had loved her schooling. Her parents had tried to give her everything they could possible, and they gave a hell of a lot.

But when the capitulation of France happened in 1940, Janet had to make a choice. She could either stay in the newly occupied regions or go into the Free zone. She was a teacher at a local girl's school and continued for a little whilst the Reich continued to consolidate its power, but when they wanted to convert the school into a base of spying operations.

Janet left.

As Janet stood by a horribly cramp little kitchen

sink made of awfully cold metal and finished washing up some potatoes for tonight's dinner. She really wondered where her life had gone, she knew she was damn well lucky to have a job at all with her being relatively free to enjoy her evening by herself.

But she missed the children, the teaching and the learning that came from being a teacher. She had of course tried to go back into teaching but it… it wasn't what it was like before.

The Nazis wanted her to teach innocent children about how grand Germany and Hilter was and how everything else was awful.

Janet couldn't do it, and now she was a maid for a good man called Reuben Portia, a wealthy businessman.

Janet didn't like the sheer coldness of the freezing water as she continued washing the potatoes that she had ever so carefully grown in the back garden over the summer and stored over the winter. She just hoped she would have enough for Christmas Day in a few weeks.

The smell of a watery tomato sauce with some scraps of leftovers from the Master's dinner was boiling away for her own dinner tonight. As much as Janet knew the Reuben would allow her to have a "real" dinner, she just didn't feel comfortable.

She had carefully heard what the Master and his strange friends had been talking about recently. The fall of Vichy, the crackdown on the French resistance networks and the increasing danger of France were all worrying.

If anything happened Janet just wanted to make sure Reuben had enough food to survive. He had given her so much when no one else wanted a simple country woman who used to teach little children.

The tiny window of cold natural light shone through behind her and Janet wished it was the summer once again so her ageing back would be warmed through before she had to finish her cleaning duties for the day.

Janet was about to get out her excuse of a chopping broad when people pounding the wooden front door echoed around the house.

Because the potatoes needed to dry and because she wanted to look very busy for Reuben, she threw the dripping wet potatoes into her apron and held the bottom of the apron to create a makeshift bag to carry them in.

Then to prevent Master from getting mad Janet swore under her breath as she walked up the little stairs to the ground floor (her little kitchen was almost buried underground in a former cellar). Then she went through the massive estate house with her ageing feet tapping on the hardwood floor as she went.

After passing plenty of very maintained and perfectly cleaned rooms filled with expensive furniture, photos and decorations that she polished each day. She made it to the very large wooden door where the pounding was coming from.

"Police!" someone shouted.

Janet carefully wiped her hands on her little apron, took a deep breath of the cold crispy air and opened the door.

She was flat out amazed all the potatoes were still in her little makeshift apron bag.

Janet had to control herself when she saw the three Gestapo German officers standing there. Their expression were as hard as a person's could get, they looked furious and like they were hunting something or something.

They easily towered over Janet.

"Yes?" Janet asked.

"We have been authorised to search this estate in search of resistance activity," the shortest of the Germans said forcing their way into the house.

Janet had no idea what he was talking about. Reuben was no resistance operative, spy or anything like that. The Germans would never find anything, they were stupid (amongst other reasons) to even consider this.

A few moments later Reuben came to the front door wearing a very expensive black suit, black shoes and carrying a black cane that was more for show than anything else.

The Germans explained what was going on, he protested and let the Germans start their search. They started with the ground floor.

Janet subtly shook her head but as the Germans started their silly searching, her eyes flicked to her

Master and he was concerned.

Janet had known Reuben long enough to know when he wasn't okay. To people who didn't know him very well then they (like the Germans) probably thought he was happy and pleasant.

But he was annoyed, concerned and probably angry.

If there was anything here then Janet just had to help him, but... the strange guests. Janet had never connected it before but what if those strange guests talking about Germany were actually resistant agents?

That made so much sense.

Janet didn't dare let that realisation show at all, but she had to do something.

Clearly Reuben had taken something in for the resistances. It wouldn't be a person because Janet was the only cook and she didn't feed anyone else, and she hadn't seen any food go missing.

It couldn't be that.

Janet seriously doubted Reuben had any secret papers, folders or anything because she cleared his office every other day. There was nothing new there.

Then Janet realised there was one place in the entire house where she wasn't allowed to go. She wasn't allowed to go in the attic, it was never locked or anything but Janet respected Reuben's wishes.

What if something was inside?

Janet subtly looked at the potatoes in her apron and the elegant wooden staircase that would take her (after a while) up to the attic. She had to go and the potatoes would just slow her down.

Equally she couldn't throw them on the ground because that would alert the Germans to what she was doing.

She had to take them with her.

As fast as she could Janet went over to the staircase and started climbing the stairs.

Normally this was an easy job despite Janet's ageing joints. But carrying all the weight of the potatoes wasn't helping her.

"Back half clear!" one of the Germans shouted.

Janet tried to hurry up. She was only halfway up to the first floor and the Germans would be moving to the second floor soon.

She had to hurry.

She kept climbing.

Janet made it to the first floor. She kept on climbing the stairs.

"Ground floor clear!" the Germans shouted.

Then Janet heard the Germans hurrying up the stairs and they immediately dived into searching the first floor.

Janet was sure her legs were about to buckle, the potatoes would be dropped and the Germans would come for her.

They didn't. Janet kept going up the stairs.

Thankfully there were only three floors and the attic in the house, but that gave Janet little comfort.

Janet made it to the second floor. Her heart was racing. She felt tired.

She continued.

"First floor cleared!"

Again the Germans raced up the stairs behind her. The second floor was the largest. It would hopefully take the longest to search.

Janet forced herself to go on. She wasn't sure how much longer she could carry the potatoes.

She made it to the third floor and she couldn't hold this many potatoes anymore. She had to waste valuable time by diving into Reuben's bedroom quickly.

Thankfully she hadn't collected the lunch plates on his desk yet. She placed some potatoes on there.

She hurried out again and went up to the attic. Janet felt so much better now without the extra kilogram or two.

When she got to the top of the stairs there was a very large brown door with a sticky handle that Janet had to try and open. The problem was the potatoes kept her hands busy.

Janet carefully tried to open the door with four fingers. It wasn't moving.

Janet had to ever, ever so carefully take the two corners of her apron that formed the made-shift bag and hold them in one hand. Giving her a hand free to open the door.

She tried with her free hand. It wasn't moving.

She pushed it.

A potato fell out. Rolling down the stairs.

Janet froze. Fears of being captured, sent to

prison and executed gripped her.

The potato rolled into Reuben's bedroom.

Janet tried to open it again. The door opened and Janet went straight inside.

Considering how big the tiny little attic looked, it was rather unimpressive as it was no bigger than ten foot by ten foot, it was covered in dust and there was only a desk by the circular window.

But Janet hated how cold and dark it was up here, she had thought she had heard a strange tapping sound coming from here some nights. Until now she hadn't given it much thought.

Janet went over to the desk and noticed the dust and the darkness had almost hidden a very large suitcase. She popped it open and gasped when she saw a wireless radio transmitter like the resistance used.

She had no clue what the different pieces did, she had just heard this was what they looked like with their little tappy-things, screens and the rest.

She had to get rid of this thing for Reuben before the Germans found it. Janet didn't know how.

Then Janet had an idea. A few years ago she had helped the old cleaner move a large wooden chest up here before the break out of the war and the old cleaner died.

Janet looked around and in a very, very dark corner she saw the very dusty chest. Because of the dust she couldn't tell or remember the colour of the chest, but that didn't matter.

She went over to the chest, opened it and almost cried in delight that the chest was empty.

"Second floor cleared!"

Janet had to hurry. She unloaded most of the potatoes because she wanted to carry the radio out of the attic. No one would suspect she was carrying or hiding it.

With most of the potatoes in the chest, she closed it and went back over to the radio transmitter. She closed the suitcase and put it carefully in her made-shift apron bag.

It was heavy!

To make matters worse, Janet had to get some more potatoes to put on top of the suitcase or it would be easy to tell what it was.

"Third floor clear!"

Janet heard the Germans race up towards her.

Janet raced over to the chest. Grabbed some potatoes. Covered up the suitcase.

She left.

As she calmly walked down the stairs she smiled and nodded to the Germans as they let her past carrying the radio transmitter.

They didn't say a word.

***

An hour later when the Germans had finished researching the house (requiring Janet to hide the transmitter in her wood store), Reuben sat quietly on a very expensive leather chair at the head of a long dining table in the middle of his most decorated room.

Janet had always loved the golden tones, the ocean blue of the wallpaper and the grand art that hung on the walls. She was allowed to sit with Reuben tonight and he was in a very, very good mood as they both sat there with their dinner.

The transmitter was right next to Janet, she had subtly bought it into the dining room when Ruben had started eating his dinner.

Janet lifted it onto the table and passed it over to Reuben.

"Your radio is very heavy Sir," Janet said.

Reuben's face lit up and smiled. Janet had never seen him so happy.

Then Janet quickly told him what she had done with the potatoes and how she had figured it out. Reuben was just shocked.

Reuben stood up and gave Janet a massive hug, something he had never done before, and he even poured her a glass of wine. The last time she had had wine was the night before France's capitulation.

"Thank you," Reuben said. "You really aren't just some simple country woman, are you?"

Janet raised her glass and they cheered each other.

As the night continued, the two loved, smiled and for the first time since the breakout of the war, Janet actually felt good about herself. She had always been worried about where her life had been leading her, but she was actually where she needed to be.

Whilst she would never get involved in her Master's resistance work, she would always protect him and make sure he was safe.

Just like he would do for her.

As the coldness of the December night set in, Janet was glad she was here tonight and not in some cold German prison waiting for her and her Master's execution.

And knowing that was all because of her made her entire year, and she just knew it was going to be a brilliant December and New Year.

PERFECT CHRISTMAS

When people ask me what my perfect Christmas is, I always have an answer for them.

My perfect Christmas is hugging with my grandchildren around a roaring warm fire with Christmas songs quietly playing in the ground all whilst I read their favourite stories to them.

That's the sort of grandma I am.

I really love my grandchildren and my own children of course, they're funny, smart and amazing. Meaning I want to be the best grandma I could to them, so when they come round tonight I'm going to make them hot rich coco with little marshmallows and let them stay up as long as they want.

That's the amazing grandma I am.

But when the police showed up and escorted me to their police car, I was not impressed. I mean how dare they interfere with my perfect Christmas.

Sure there's the body of an unfortunate soul on my living room floor, but I need to start making the hot coco for my grandchildren before they turn up.

But as I sit here with my ancient back against the cold hard plastic of the seat, I'm starting to doubt that will ever happen. Now mind you, I honestly wouldn't mind this but the police car smells awful. It smells of cheesy feet and not like the amazing Christmas spices coming from my kitchen.

I also baked my grandchildren a heavenly Christmas cake, but I still need to ice it and marzipan it for them.

Forcing my mind away from the number of problems I was facing (my darling late Jasper always said I needed to be more organised), I turned my attention to the view of my little house outside the car.

There were tall handsome police men and women walking in and out of my house like they owned the place, I wished I had made them cookies now. And I really, really hoped they weren't going to crush any of my winter flowers that lined the small pathway up to my house from the street.

It took me and Jasper years to get those flowers to, well, flower each and every winter like clockwork. Oh and the grandchildren loved them. I hope the police are careful.

With all the watching of the police people almost crush my flowers starting to give me heart problems (at this rate I'm going to miss the time I take my heart meds), I wondered about some of the weird questions the police were asking me.

Now, I don't know why, but why is whenever a body is found in the house of a little old lady do they presume I'm mad or strange?

I have never seen that body before. I only had a quick look before I called the police, I think it was a man, probably young, but I didn't recognise him.

Then you had all the rude police officers

questioning me like I should magically know who it was because they were in my house. It's just typical that the police think like that, well, if they keep interfering with my perfect Christmas plans I'm going to have to say something.

This was outrageous!

A few moments later the car doors opened, slammed shut and the engine started as I saw two policemen sitting in front. The taller man to my left looked at me whilst the other shorter one stared at me in the rearview mirror.

On normal days I'm sure these officers are great people, but for Christ's sake (I'm not sorry for swearing!) why are they interrogating me. I have Christmas cakes to ice and marzipan and I need to make the coco!

After some more moments of silence I decided enough was enough. I am a grandma I have to do what's right for my family.

"Officers, I'm sure this is all a misunderstanding. I need to do things for my grandchildren. You know it's Christmas. You know my family's coming later on. I need to finish everything,"

When I saw the two officers look at each other and smiled, I was shocked. Shocked I tell you. Here I was trying to be there for my family and these two men who probably weren't even old enough to have families were judging me. Judging me of all people!

If I had my handbag with me I would hit them, and yes I am so that sort of old lady.

"Sorry Miss but we need to take you down town,"

I raised my hands to my chest. That poor soul, he must have been murdered or something and the police need my help. That is so nice of them to recognise my importance, you know I actually tried to be a policewoman once, but back then it was so sexist I left. At least I finally get my chance to prove myself.

"Of course officers. Anything you need I'm sure I can help,"

Again the two officers looked at each other, probably agreeing how important I was. Maybe there weren't so bad after all.

***

Maybe I was completely wrong!

I have been stuck in this tiny little interrogation room with ugly black walls, a massive mirror and two chairs for over an hour. What's worse is the entire place smells of horrid cleaning chemicals. What I wouldn't give to be in my wonderfully Christmas scented kitchen right now.

This is stupid.

My grandchildren and my own kids could be standing outside my place in the freezing cold waiting for me. That is just terrible, they must think I'm a terrible grandma, oh I would hate that. I am not a bad grandma.

Taking another horrid breath of those harsh chemicals that made my tongue taste disgusting lemons (I hate lemons with a passion), I noticed how cold the room was.

What did they want? Their people to freeze to death, I wanted to help them with my brilliance, not freeze to death.

Then I saw the two officers from earlier open and close the door behind me and walk around like I was some cheap meal for these two hungry predators.

With the light being so much better than that

awful car, I focused on each officer for a moment. The taller officer was terribly handsome with his dark hair, slim body and perfect jawline. Just like my Jasper was before he died.

But the other one, bless his heart, was pig ugly. No actually, I'm being terribly harsh, he was beautiful to someone. Just not me. With his horse-like face and massive teeth and short hair.

Again not my cup of tea, but I'm sure he'll find someone.

But I have to say the horse faced one did remind me of a neighbour, no sorry, a neighbour's kid that normally checks on me and even does some shopping for me from time to time. Terribly great kid.

In fact I thought he was meant to come round tonight because one of my grandchildren, I know, she's getting on to about eighteen and her brothers are a lot younger. But I still wanted to do the whole perfect Christmas and everything with her, yet I wanted her to meet this neighbour's kid.

You see a grandma always has an eye for love and I think they would make a perfect couple. She's eighteen. He's twenty-one. Perfect.

I must remember to introduce them at some point.

"Miss, are you okay?" Horse-faced asked me.

I shook my head as I realised I must have been in deep thought.

"I'm sorry officer. I was thinking about my grandchildren. Will this take long? I must get back to them,"

The two officers smiled and nodded at each other.

"Miss do you know the man in your kitchen?"

the handsome officer asked.

I shook my head. "No of course not. But I hope he didn't suffer,"

The handsome officer sat down in the chair opposite me.

"I'm afraid that was Mr Tyler Oddlong,"

I gave a friendly smile to the officer but that didn't ring any bells.

Horse-faced knelt down next to me. "According to your neighbours, he came to see you regularly,"

I nodded. "Oh I'm sorry. I just remember him as the neighbour kid,"

Oh damn. That poor kid, I needed him to meet my granddaughter and he was such a good kid, so caring, loving and respectful.

"Did you kill him?" the handsome officer asked.

"I did not!" I shouted.

How the hell could the police think that?

I'm… I'm a good grandma.

I opened my mouth to protest my innocent but my mind went blank and I remembered seeing Tyler earlier. He was smiling, telling me about his Christmas plans then nothing.

"Do you own a rolling pin?" Horse-faced asked.

I nodded as a memory of me gently hitting the palm of my hand with the rolling pin earlier… when Tyler was there.

"I did not kill him," I said, my voice starting to break.

But I couldn't have killed him, I am a great grandma. What grandparents do you know who does so much for their family? I am going to make a perfect Christmas for my kids and my grandchildren.

It will be… a memory of me talking to Tyler

about my granddaughter entered my mind and he wasn't happy. He respectfully declined to meet her, saying he already had a girlfriend, so I protested.

I raised my hands to my face as I realised what happened. I kept pressing Tyler, I wasn't happy, Tyler wanted to leave and I picked up the rolling pin.

But I will have the perfect Christmas.

I simply smiled at the two officers who must have been expecting me to crack or something judging by the look on their faces.

"Please officers. Unless you have any proof I must get back to my house. I have a Christmas cake to ice, marzipan and coco to make,"

The two officers just shook their heads and the handsome officer left.

With Horse-faced following him, he turned back to me before he left and simply said:

"I'm sorry Miss. It isn't Christmas at all. It's March and your family aren't coming this time. Maybe they can visit you in prison,"

When the door slammed shut, I actually smiled as I started to plan my perfect Christmas in prison, because to me the perfect Christmas with me, my children and my grandchildren was the only thing that really mattered.

No matter who got in the way.

AUTHOR OF THE BETTIE ENGLISH PRIVATE MYSTERIES

CONNOR WHITELEY

CRIMINAL RESISTANCE ALLIANCE

A WORLD WAR TWO HISTORICAL MYSTERY SHORT STORY

CRIMINAL, RESISTANCE, ALLIANCE
16th December 1942
Correze, France

French Resistance Leader Mary Tencade would never let any of her agents know it but she did love the stunning area of Correze, even if it was the dead of winter. She only wanted them to believe that her sole focus was on what she did best, running Alliance.

She still couldn't believe she was alive, running the largest resistance network in France and she was still free. There had been so many close-calls of late and she hated to know what laid ahead.

But for now Mary just wanted to enjoy the stunning view of Correze from the little window of the abandoned chateau she was in.

It definitely wasn't the best one she had stayed in but it was far from the worse. The chateau hadn't seen any love, attention or respect for decades with its constant ugly layer of dust, dirt and Mary seriously didn't want to consider what else was there.

But it would serve its purpose.

It was the perfect spot for a little break away and hiding spot for a few weeks until she could decide what to do next. It was the most perfect isolated spot in south central France with its wildest and rockiness that made sure very few Germans came here.

They probably thought no sane person or resistance group would dare set up in this most awful place. But Mary didn't agree, its wildness, cold temperatures and isolation made it perfect.

Granted she still had to find somewhere for her radio operative to set up so he could get a clear signal to MI6 in London. But that could definitely wait a little while, she just wanted to enjoy the stunning view out of her bedroom in the chateau.

The wonderfully cold yet fresh air was such a pleasant change from the harsh-smelling air from the German vehicles in the cities and other occupied parts of France that left the taste of foul smoke on her tongue. She would never really be able to stand at a window too much in any other place.

In fact she probably shouldn't be standing here now, so she slowly closed the window shutters, went over to her somewhat soft double bed and just fell onto it.

The world was turning into such a crazy place. More of her agents had been arrested, imprisoned and killed in recent weeks and months. Beautiful, sexy Faerun wasn't back yet and Mary would never admit it to anyone but him, but she did love him.

When she started off in this resistance work with her friend Narave she honestly didn't believe she would be able to do any of this. There were still some days she felt like she couldn't, or she was just kidding herself that her network was important to the war effort.

They were all just amateur spies after all.

Yet there was just something about Faerun with his beautiful body, charisma and… he was just perfect to help run Alliance, work with MI6 and to have as a partner in life. Mary wanted so badly to have him back for Christmas, she knew that might not happen.

The gentle sound of the biting wind blowing outside was so strange to hear after years of constantly tapping of radio transmitters, talking and shouting of her headquarter staff and the inevitable German that was far too commonplace for Mary's liking.

She wanted to change that, but it wouldn't change anytime soon.

Especially with the damn Nazis having invaded Vichy, the so-called independent (more like puppet) free zone of France where the Nazis didn't apparently rule. That happened on the 10th of November, but it just felt like yesterday.

Mary buried herself into her sheets more and more in some pointless attempt to give her some calming comfort. She had loved escaping the police station her and her friends were prisoners in from the help of Anti-Germany Vichy police officers, but she hated that the Germans invaded Vichy the night before.

She would never forget the amazing braveness of those police officers, who wanted to help her and her friends stay alive and support the war effort.

Out of everything going on in the country, Europe and world that was probably what kept her going the most. Mary had always been amazed by the amount of support of people got in the most dire of situations. She knew exactly how lucky she was, most resistant groups didn't get that lucky, but that's what drove her.

She knew how many of those amazing people got caught, imprisoned and executed for helping her and her agents. So she was damn well going to repay the favour and help all of France get free as soon as she could.

That just seemed impossible now with the Vichy police, army and everything else all over France falling into Nazi hands and becoming nothing more than monsters for Hilter.

The number of friends for resistance groups was running out. Fast.

Footsteps came from downstairs.

Mary shot up.

She carefully tried to listen to the voices that were walking about and talking as they did so.

German.

Damn it!

From what Mary could hear there were at least

three Germans downstairs walking about the chateau.

Mary wanted to run, but there was nowhere to go. She had sent her agents out to get some food for the Christmas celebrations and other guests she had coming in a few days.

She was alone.

Mary grabbed the revolver from under her pillow.

She was going hunting.

No Germans were killing her.

***

After carefully tip-toeing down the long, but awfully narrow stone staircase, Mary crouched down and peeked round the corner to spy on her evil visitors. She was surprised how quickly the visitors had managed to make it into the heart of the chateau.

The large meeting room was easily twenty metres long with two large fireplaces carved right into the walls, a long oak table that Mary looked forward to eating round in a few days time was in the middle and a large suitcase was on top.

Mary wanted to rush out and grab the suitcase that was filled with intelligence reports, questionnaires and other things that MI6 had sent her recently.

It might have sounded careless to just leave the suitcase on the table, but Mary had hardly expected to be suddenly attacked by Germans and her staff were only meant to be gone for a little while.

It was a stupid mistake but one she was determined to correct.

The horrible smell of sweat, body odour and dead body made Mary carefully look at the four Germans who were inspecting the meeting room.

They thankfully didn't have the uniform, arrogance or sheer aura of death that came from Gestapo officers, but Mary still didn't want to take any chances.

Then she noticed the dead man on her floor next to one of the fireplaces in the middle of the room. The man was definitely French, probably a blacksmith judging by his rather good muscles, blackened face and the odd burn on his hands.

Mary was hardly impressed that these Germans might not have been spies or secret police but they were definitely killers. They were probably in here trying to find a place to hide the body.

Something she couldn't have anywhere near here.

From reports she had gotten from other resistance networks, having dead bodies about end ever ended well.

One of her friends had killed a German infiltrator and buried him in the garden. The wildlife was drawn to it and it wasn't long until the police turned up and the resistance network fell.

Mary was not letting that happen.

She focused on the four Germans and noticed how they were all carrying the same type of pistol. All Nazi standard issue, they were probably soldiers stationed in a nearby base, but this was Correze, miles away from any type of Nazi base.

These soldiers were probably rogues or something.

And in Mary's experience rogues were just as dangerous, if not more so, than the loyal monsters.

The Germans started muttering to themselves again and Mary noticed a long cast iron fire poker was leaning against the fireplace. It wasn't hard to get to but she would have to be quick.

Mary hardly wanted to use a gun if she could help it because they were far too loud and then any Gestapo units nearby would definitely come running.

She couldn't risk that.

The four Germans walked over to the dead body and stood around him talking and gesturing to the fireplace.

Mary couldn't believe they were actually thinking about burning the body. They clearly didn't know how awful of a smell of that was, it would attract everyone from here to Paris and Marseille.

It was suicide.

Thankfully, Mary knew more than a little German (it helped in coding secret messages and hearing what the enemy were thinking) to get by so she was going to have to risk herself to save her network once again.

She hid her pistol in her back pocket.

"Do you speak French?" she asked, stepping out from the stairs.

The four Germans spun around. Their guns pointed at her.

"We do," the tallest German said.

His short well-styled blond hair and blue eyes almost made Mary laugh. He must have been popular in the military.

"Burning a body will not help you. It causes too much of a smell. A smell that will attract police officers," Mary said calmly.

The Germans sneered at her.

They cocked their pistols.

"What are you? Resistance? British?" the tallest one said.

Mary was almost offended. How dare he think of her as British! As much as she loved the British, MI6 and everything they had given her, she was French to the core. She did all of this so France could be free once more.

She was not British.

"I am a woman who wants to live in peace," Mary said coldly.

The four German people took a step closer and started looking her up and down.

Mary seriously wanted her staff to get back soon.

Mary carefully walked over to the fireplace and made soon the fire poker was within reach if she needed it.

"She's a woman indeed," the tallest man said.

Mary was definitely going to kill him first and foremost.

"Who was the dead man?" Mary asked.

The Germans spat on the corpse behind them.

Mary was tempted to act with them being distracted but that man might be important to someone.

"Just a resistance git who asked too many questions about troop movements. Alliance scum," the tallest man said.

Mary forced herself not to react. The man must have been one of the new recruits that she hadn't met yet.

As much as it pained it about the casual recruitment process of those outside her inner circle, she didn't have an alternative. She still hated losing her agents, even if she didn't know that.

These Germans had to pay.

Mary went for the fire poker. She grabbed it. Swinging it.

The poker smashed into the Germans.

Killing the tallest one instantly.

His blood splashed against the table.

The Germans were shocked. They froze. Mary did not.

She swung it again.

Shattering the skull of another.

Mary rammed it into the head of the third one.

The last German tackled her.

Punching her in the face.

Mary swung the poker again.

It smashed into his chest.

He fell off her.

Mary climbed on top of him.

Smashing the poker through his eye.

A few moments later five men and women ran into the room carrying paper shopping bags, food and weapons. They were shocked to see Mary covered in blood and the corpses around her.

Mary didn't have time to welcome them back. They had to clear up.

"Go back into town carefully," Mary said. "Get some lye. We have bodies to clear up,"

***

25th December 1942
Correze, France

To Mary's utter relief, it had been more than easy for her staff to secretly buy from lye in the local town and as soon as they got back Mary and the others had made sure to dissolve the bodies. A neat trick she had learnt from the British.

As the other sector leaders and agents had turned up and joined her for the Christmas gathering, she had warned them about the bodies and the possible risk they posed to them all.

They had all plotted out escape routes and everyone had agreed that Mary was the most important person who had to escape. Mary loved that dedication but she loved her agents and friends more.

To her very pleasant surprise Faerun had returned on the 17th and that lead to a very pleasurable night and it was wonderful to hear what adventures he had been on in Algiers. And Mary was really looking forward to seeing him again for a little longer.

As Mary sat at the head at the large oak table surrounded by fine food, wine and even finer friends, she just couldn't believe how lucky she was that she was finally able to relax for a little bit and just be a normal person.

A person that could socialise, laugh and just have fun for one day of the year before getting back to constantly running, hiding and intelligence work.

The smell of freshly roasted succulent chicken was intoxicating when combined with the hints of rosemary and thyme that a local shopkeeper had stored from the summer just for them.

And everyone continued their eating, celebrating and Christmas drinking, Mary just smiled at Faerun. The beautiful man who helped her run it all, and the man she truly loved.

It might be the close of one great year, and Mary might have been completely fearful about what was to come in 1943, but she knew she could do anything with the amazing people round the table by her side.

And that simply delighted her.

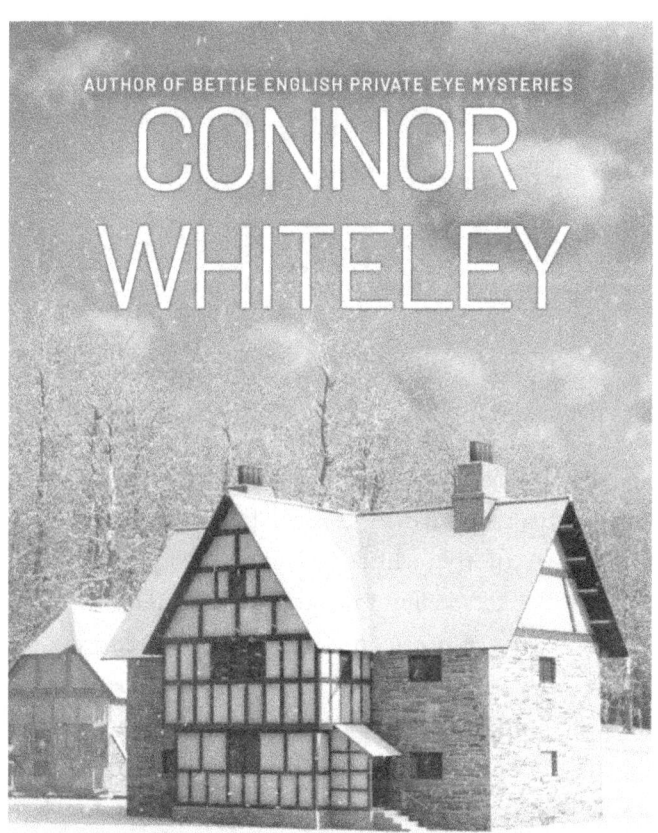

DARKFARM

Farm Boy Tyler Gray stood on the freezing cold dirt road surrounded by endless fields buried under a thick layer of the whitest of snow that looked like endless blankets veiling the land with his family's farm Tudor-style farmhouse in the middle of the farm.

Tyler continued to stand there in the dirt road as he watched his father's wooden wagon ride off into the distance. His father had said he was going away for a few days in hope of selling some of the last grain, potatoes and chicken that the family had from this year's harvest.

Tyler just hoped his father would make it back in time for Christmas.

The forecast had promised there to be another two snowstorms, which for England was a rarity in its own right, so Tyler was seriously starting to doubt if his precious father would come back in time for Christmas.

He couldn't imagine anything worse than being

stuck with his mother, two sisters and little brother for Christmas. His mother was an awful woman, loud, abusive and just foul.

Thankfully she had been okay recently, happy even, but Tyler and his eldest sister Franny knew that would change in an instance.

The only thing Tyler could do now was wait, and if any trouble did come up, he had to be the man of the house now and protect his siblings.

As it was only morning, and a damn cold one at that, Tyler and his siblings had enough chores to do that all of them should be able to avoid their mother for most of the day. Tyler would have liked to just get rid of her entirely but he wasn't sure his father would like that.

As much as Tyler absolutely loved his father for his laughter, kindness and patience. He was as blind as a tree to his wife's cruelness. Tyler had tried to tell him so many times about what his mother had done to his sisters, but his father never believed him.

And every single time that happened it killed Tyler inside. He wanted to protect his sisters, but he was nothing more than a failure in that department.

When Tyler could no longer see his father's wagon, he sadly started to walk back towards the farmhouse. It was a great walk actually, Tyler loved seeing the endless amount of snow that perfectly covered the land.

It was like he was living in a winter wonderland.

After a few minutes, Tyler walked past the little

outhouses, wooden storage sheds and a rather tall windmill that was meant to make power for the farm, but it had been broken for years.

Next year Tyler was going to fix it up, no matter how much that mother of his protested. She didn't get a voice in how the farm was run.

Tyler went to the large wooden door in the Tudor-style farmhouse that led to the kitchen. Tyler smiled and was filled with relief at the sight of the multiple pieces of string attached to the door were still intact.

The string was one of the most important things on the farm in his opinion. It allowed them to survive and navigate the farm despite how bad the storm was.

The string had saved Tyler's life more than once.

Tyler went into the large brown kitchen with its little-brown worktops lining the outside, the large gas stove and sink against the far edge of the kitchen, and to Tyler's complete surprise his youngest brother and sister were sitting round the wooden table smiling, laughing and eating a freshly cooked breakfast.

It smelt amazing with its fresh hints of sausages, bacon and eggs that filled the entire kitchen. It smelt like a home filled with love, respect and admiration. Tyler was definitely going to have to thank Fanny for cooking the breakfast for them.

"Tyler!" his mother shouted as her overweight body stomped across the kitchen and hugged him.

Tyler was filled with horror at the idea of his mother loving him and being in a good mood. Her breath stunk of whiskey. His father had promised Tyler before he left that all the whiskey was gone but clearly his mother had hidden more bottles somewhere.

Tyler gave his mother a quick kiss on the forehead, smiled and then carefully went over to Fanny who was standing in the kitchen doorway that led into the living room at the other end of the kitchen near the stove.

Tyler was impressed to see Fanny in her jeans, red and green t-shirt and jumper. She looked good, but Tyler could see how worried she was about the breakfast and everything.

This wasn't going to end well.

They both knew that.

The only problem with being the oldest at 20 of the family was that Tyler just felt like everything was down to him these days. It didn't matter that Fanny was 18, his youngest sister was 14 and his brother was 12.

Tyler was still nervous as hell because of it.

As much as Tyler wanted to stay and watch the breakfast and jump in if he was needed. He did have jobs to do and if he was going from past experience, him just being there and watching built-up tensions.

So if he left he might be doing everyone a favour.

The sound of the wind howling outside made Tyler fold his arms. There was a snowstorm now.

Tyler went over to his foul mother and hugged her.

"Thanks for doing this mum," he said.

His mother smiled. "Course dear. Happy to. Are you going to work today?"

"Yea, dad wanted me to check some of the outhouses," Tyler said.

His mother kissed and hugged him and then smiled.

"You wrap up warm little one. Stay safe," she said.

Tyler smiled and kissed her again on the head then he put on his massively coat, (fake) fur-lined boots and went outside.

As Tyler was surprised at the snowstorm was as heavy as it was, he couldn't see the outhouses, the broken windmill or the fields anymore. They were all covered in a shroud of snow, but Tyler wasn't going to the outhouses. He wanted to check on the broken windmill.

He was now starting to believe that if he could repair it before his father got home then it would be a perfect Christmas present to the whole family on the big day.

Tyler found the piece of string that led to the windmill and he followed it carefully. He didn't risk falling over in case he pulled and broke the string. Then he would be a dead man.

But Tyler wasn't going to deny that his mother's sweet nature this morning wasn't concerning him. It was great when she was like that, and that was why Tyler always made sure he got enough love and attention to last him until his mother was like that again (in another year).

Yet when she did turn, she was always so horrible, foul and even worse than usual. Tyler didn't want to be out for too long, just in case his mother did turn on them.

After a few minutes of struggling through the snow, Tyler walked into the freezing cold wooden door of the broken windmill. He couldn't even see the door that was how bad the storm was, and he couldn't even hear himself think. The howling was so bad.

Tyler forced open the door to the windmill and shot inside.

The smell of whiskey, bourbon and stale beer was overwhelming. And when Tyler really focused on the large box room after recovering from the shock of the warmer room, he was disgusted at the amount of empty and full whiskey bottles he saw.

No one wonder his mother had protested so much to him coming in here. This was where she was hiding everything she shouldn't have in the first place.

Tyler wanted to smash them all up, but that would probably just make things worse.

She might think that one of his sisters or young brother came in here and smashed them. She might attack, harm and abuse them like she normally did.

No.

Tyler couldn't do anything about the bottles until his father was bad safe and sound. Then Tyler would smash the bottles (or steal them and sell them in the town for a bit of money). Then if his mother turned abusive, his father could finally see.

After about an hour of checking out the windmill, its upper floors and its electricals, Tyler just laughed at himself for even thinking he could do it alone in a few days.

It was a much larger job than that but he had a pretty good idea about what to do, so he could tell his father his plan and they could hopefully do it together.

They would both love that.

Tyler went back out of the windmill, grabbed the string and went back to the kitchen door. When he went inside, the smell of sausages, bacon and eggs was long gone, and Tyler just felt like you could cut the tension with a knife.

Tyler quietly took off his boots and coat and went into the large living room, with its massive Christmas tree, red sofas and roaring fireplace where Fanny was holding the two youngest children who were screaming and crying their eyes out.

Tyler was just furious. He wanted to shout and demand an explanation from his mother, but then he heard a massive door slam.

That was exactly what his mother always did as soon as he came in. She always locked herself away in her room.

Tyler went over to Fanny and lovingly took his little brother from her, cradling him in his arms.

"What happened?" Tyler asked quietly.

Fanny shrugged. "These two asked about going out to build a snowman. She flipped out and punched them both,"

Tyler just held his brother tight. There was no reason to hurt them, all she needed to do was tell them it wasn't safe with the storm.

Tyler kept hugging his brother and just wished his mother was no longer about. But he was starting to get worried about his father, did he make it to town before the storm?

Was he going to make it back for the big day?

Was he ever coming back?

Fanny moved closer to Tyler and they all just sat there in silence, comforting and supporting each other. Tyler had always known Fanny was a great caring mother, and her own kids when she was older were going to be extremely lucky.

But Tyler just wanted his father to hurry up and return.

***

For the rest of the day, Tyler and Fanny and the two youngest children laughed, sang and told stories in the living room next to the roaring fire. It was the most fun Tyler had had for ages, it was amazing what having real family time could do for a person.

Then as the day got late, Tyler and Fanny went into their bedrooms and bought out the duvets and pillows so they could all sleep in front of the protective warmth of the fire tonight.

They had all been sleeping for hours when it struck midnight and Tyler heard someone moving about the house. He carefully looked up from his makeshift bed and saw the bulk of his mother slip into the kitchen.

Tyler then heard the kitchen door open.

As much as he wanted to talk to his mother, he knew that wouldn't change anything.

Tyler silently got up, he didn't bother to put on any of his warm clothing. He just opened the door, felt the pieces of string that shot off from the house until he felt a piece tighter than the others.

He had to force his very cold self not to laugh in the slightest when he knew his mother was going to the windmill. The storm at this point was the worse Tyler had ever seen, he couldn't even see his hand that was only about twenty centimetres away.

Tyler untied the string. It fell to the floor. Then Tyler locked the kitchen for good measure.

His mother was going to freeze to death.

Thankfully.

***

After making a wonderfully light, refreshing breakfast of some preserved fruits and homemade yoghurt for the young ones, Tyler and Fanny both stood at the little kitchen window and stared at the perfectly calm morning.

The sun was shining more than Tyler had seen in months, even the temperature was surprisingly pleasant, and right in the middle of the farm and windmill was a frozen and very dead woman.

Their mother was finally dead and the abuse could stop.

Tyler would never tell his family what he did, and he just knew they didn't care but Fanny just hugged him so tight.

"Thank you," she whispered.

Tyler just shrugged. At the end of the day, Tyler was just doing what he thought was right for himself, his family and his father. But they were all free now to enjoy life without the constant threat of her abuse.

"You know she was scared of you," Fanny said.

Tyler just smiled. It would explain why she never came out of her room after she abused his siblings, and maybe she was right to be scared of him. He did, after all, kill her.

But she never should have abused his family in the first place.

The sound of crunching snow made all four siblings race to put on their coats and boots and they ran out of the farmhouse.

Their daddy was home.

Tyler just felt so pleased that his father was back safe and sound, and as he climbed down from his wagon and petted the horse. He saw the body of his wife, and looked at Tyler.

Tyler felt his heart jump to his throat. Was his father about to shout and disown him?

Was his father about to hit him?

Was his father about to leave them all forever?

Instead his father just gave him a sad smile when he saw the two massive bruises on the youngest siblings' faces, and he hugged Tyler.

"I'm so sorry," his father said.

Tyler just hugged him back tight because his father wasn't mad at him or his siblings. He loved them because he was a good father, a damn good one.

And with Christmas in just a few days, Tyler couldn't wait to spend it with his real family. His siblings and father that actually loved, cared and wanted the best for each other.

Because today wasn't a sad day. It was a day that marked the beginning of a new start for all of them, the start of being free from an abuser and Tyler was really, really looking forward to how great that was going to feel.

CRIMINAL CHRISTMAS VOLUME 2

GREAT GIVE AWAY

Bettie English, Private Eye, loved her mother's birthday. It was always an amazing day filled with laughter, love and plenty of tasty food. But as she stood on the pavement of a long road with little houses lining each side of it, she was hardly impressed.

She had told her boyfriend, who was currently bent over the engine of her red car, to take a right then a left. That wasn't hard. It was easy, she had done it hundreds of times and her sister had done it drunk even more times.

But no. Her boyfriend Detective Graham had to take left then right, leading them to this God forsaken little road (Street?) with pretty little houses far away from her mother's house and then the car broken down.

Bettie was not impressed!

She didn't even know if Graham knew anything about cars. He was a detective, he was amazing at his job, but as she had learnt way too many times recently if she told him to put his mind to anything else, he was sexy and hot as hell, but next to useless.

Bettie had to admit watching Graham in his tight jeans, white shirt and blue shoes bend over her car was probably the only upside of the situation. Yet Bettie was starting to realise that they were going to be stuck here for a while and she hoped, prayed, whatever-ed that her mother's birthday cake wasn't going to spoil.

Granted it was cold enough. Late December was always cold in southeast England and all the little houses were covered in a thin layer of ice, frost and even a little snow, but Bettie didn't like how her breath condensed into long columns of vapour.

The smell of wonderfully warming spices filled the air and Bettie loved those smells as she remembered the buttery, luxurious mince pies she had eaten all over Christmas along with the fruity, boozy cake and yule logs. It really had been the perfect Christmas with her family and now she wanted to top it off with the perfect birthday for her mother, but that clearly wasn't going to happen within the next hour.

The sound of panicked voices in the distance made Bettie wonder what was going on. It was clear the voices were coming from further down the street, and considering Bettie had nothing better to do and Graham would never call the breakdown services, she had no other choice than to check out the sound.

And it meant Graham wouldn't be able to spring up the conversation of having kids on her again, like he had accidentally done that morning.

A conversation she really didn't want today. Especially as her mother was going to ask about it a thousand times already.

"Gra, I'm going down the street to check down

the sounds. Be back soon. Love you," Bettie said, walking down the street.

"Love you too Bet," Graham said.

Bettie actually looked at the houses as she went down the street, they were more beautiful than her quick glance had showed her earlier. Each house still had up their wide range of Christmas lights in all their different stunning colours. They were rather beautiful. Each one could probably be described as an art piece with how each house had shaped, decorated and sequenced their lights.

But why were the lights on at nine o'clock in the morning? It was hardly dark.

"The Gift is stolen!"

Bettie stared at the man who kept shouting the same thing over and over. She wasn't sure what to make of the man, he wasn't very tall, but his (hideously) bright Christmas jumper and trousers spoke volumes.

"Bettie English, Private Eye, can I help you?" she asked.

"Oh yes, you can," the man turned towards the rest of the street. "Everyone! The Great Give Away is saved!"

Bettie really didn't understand what was going on. At this rate she'll have to charge a confusion fee to these people.

As more and more people walked out of their houses towards Bettie, she couldn't believe how they all looked so different. Each person was a different height, weight and class. That alone was different from the rest of England.

"Miss? Who are you?" a little old lady said pulling on Bettie's arm.

Bettie introduced herself and wasn't sure what to make of the little old lady as her face lit up like a Christmas tree.

"Miss, the Great Give Away is lost without you?"

Now Bettie wished she had had that second mug of coffee like Graham had wanted her to. Damn him for being right!

"Sorry. What is the Great Give Away?" Bettie asked.

Everyone in the street gasped and looked at horror at Bettie.

"It's the most amazing time of the year!" everyone shouted.

The little old lady placed a cold hand on Bettie's shoulder.

"Miss. Every year on this day, we Give Away all our Christmas leftovers to the homeless so they may get fed through the New Year after our Christmas joy,"

That was a rather good idea actually, Bettie had never thought of that before. It made perfect sense and she was a bit surprised that no one else had thought of it. Everyone always bought too much at Christmas (that alone was disgusting) and everyone just threw it away (including her), but giving it to the homeless and less fortunate, now that was an excellent idea.

But the idea of someone stealing it was monstrous. Who in their right mind would steal from such a great idea?

It was probably as far from the Christmas spirit that you could get. Especially given the entire idea of St Nick and Father Christmas was to give the poor presents and help others. This theft was flat outrageous!

Bettie had to find out who did it.

The little old lady and everyone else grabbed Bettie and pulled her further down the street.

Bettie tried to resist but she just went along with it in the end.

Then the crowd pushed her in front of a large metal cage with red, pink and green tinsel covering it. But there was one very disturbing thing that caught Bettie's eyes, where a presumably large metal padlock should have been, there was only bend twisted metal.

"Is this where you stored the leftovers?" Bettie asked.

Another massive gasp from the crowd.

The little old lady gestured for the crowd to go away and leave her and Bettie alone.

"Miss. I'm sorry about that. For them The Great Give Away is the highlight of the year, they believe everyone should do it,"

"I do agree. Tell me what happened?"

"I run the street Miss. I own most of it and now walk up and down every morning and evening if my old body allows me. I walked past this morning to see the food was gone,"

"Was it there last night?" Bettie asked.

"Oh yes Miss. I bought some leftover… I mean The Gift of My Husband's Christmas Cake to donate,"

Bettie smiled. "It's okay. Say whatever you want to me, I won't get offended,"

"Thank you Miss,"

Bettie knelt down on the cold ground, looking at the twisted metal. It was clear that the lock had been forced off but that wasn't what bothered Bettie so much.

Now she was on the ground, Bettie saw stains of coffee, tea and syrups, but they were all going in the direction of the back of the cage. Not the front.

Bettie would have imagined if the thief had broken off the lock, then they would have pulled all the goods and leftovers through the front and presumably onto whatever they were using to transport the food away.

In fact the ground was cold, perfectly soft and perfectly intact. There were no impressions of feet or wheelbarrow marks or anything else that would suggest someone had been standing here weighted down with all the leftovers.

Something wasn't right here.

Bettie went round to the back of the metal cage.

"Here," Bettie said.

"What Miss?"

Bettie just pointed to the deep marks and the stains of tea, coffee and syrups in the mud.

"Oh Miss!" the little old lady said, her voice panicked.

Bettie tapped the back of the metal cage a few times and watched it vibrate, hum and eventually fall off.

"Someone must have carefully cut off the back part, stole the leftovers and twisted the lock off to make you think that was how the theft happened,"

"Oh dear Miss, oh dear. What will I do?"

Bettie stood up and placed a gentle hand on the old lady.

"Relax. It will be okay. I will find your leftovers for you. But can I ask a favour?"

"Anything Miss!"

Bettie smiled. "There's a little red car up the street with a hot man failing to fix my engine. Do you have a mechanic on the street please?"

Again the old lady's eyes lit up and she simply walked away.

Bettie had no idea if that meant they had a mechanic, or if the old lady had simply gone off to check out Graham. It sounded silly, but in Bettie's past experience the older women of the world did enjoy his looks. Thankfully she was younger than him by a few years.

Bettie knelt down next to the marks in the soft mud. They didn't look right or what she had seen from other thefts in her years as a private eye.

The marks were too narrow to be car wheels and she doubted anyone could get a car on the soft mud and get it off again without the car spinning out. Then again the marks were still too large to belong to a wheelbarrow.

And judging by the size of the metal cage and the odd marks of rice pudding on the top of it, Bettie was sure the cage had been stuffed full.

But the marks did go away from the metal cage towards one of the little houses who had a large brown fence.

Bettie went up to the fence and strangely enough the marks seemed to go straight under the fence like it wasn't there.

Maybe it hadn't?

Jumping out Bettie grabbed onto the top of the fence and pulled herself up, she'd forgotten how tough climbing was. In the new year she had to get back to the gym and do weight training, forget cardio, she had to do the weights!

Over the fence, Bettie didn't like the plainness of the little garden that she was looking at. All the garden had in it was a child's swing, a sandpit and a bed of half-dead flowers.

It all looked so plain and unloved. Unlike her garden, this one didn't scream love, nature or beauty. It looked like some half-ass attempt to make a garden fit for a family.

But the marks weren't in the garden.

"Can I help ya?" a woman said.

Bettie dropped down from the fence.

The woman in front of her was hardly a looker with her long twisted hair, short stocky body and black teeth, but Bettie had dealt with worse looking people.

"Yes actually. Did you-"

"Leave woman. I donna have time for ya. Go away and don't come back," the woman said starting to leave.

"Does your kid want a new bike?" Bettie said, randomly.

The woman stopped. "Go away. My kid don't want anything from a posh snob like you. Now leave,"

"How about some Gifts from The Great Give Away?"

The woman hissed at Bettie as she almost went into her house.

"Those snobs donna give me any. I might be poor, but I gotten a house. Now leave. I don't want ya charity,"

The door slammed shut and Bettie wasn't sure what to make of it. The woman was clearly annoyed at the street, snobs that lived here (even though Bettie had met snobs and these people weren't ones) and hated the Great Give Away.

But the woman had seen contempt at least a little bit to live her life how she wanted, Bettie doubted the woman wanted to do any harm to the world.

Bettie went over to the woman's door and pushed a twenty-pound note through the letterbox. At least the woman might be able to buy herself and her kids some food and maybe a nice treat with it.

The sound of a bike's bell made Bettie look at the street as she saw two young children ride around.

She still didn't know if she wanted kids, Graham definitely did, but he was a detective, she was a private eye. Full time jobs and lifestyles that didn't allow for kids, but she still had time to find out, if that's what she wanted.

Then Bettie looked at the tyres on the bikes, they were narrow, smaller than a car and wheelbarrow. They might be able to make the marks in the soft mud.

Bettie went over to the side of the road and knelt down.

"Kids," Bettie said, waving them over.

"Mum said don't talk to strangers!" one of the kids said, he was probably about ten.

Bettie rolled her eyes. "I'm a friend of the… little old lady, owns some of the houses,"

She had no idea if they would know who she was talking about.

"Mrs Birchwood!" the younger kid shouted, he was certainly six years old.

The ten year old kid got off his bike and walked over to Bettie, keeping at least three metres between himself and her. Very clever, Bettie was going to have to remember that if she had kids. Three metres was more than enough space to run away if she wanted to kidnap him.

Of course she didn't, but still.

"Are you two the only ones with bikes in the street?" Bettie asked.

"Na. Jonny boy has a big bikey for big boys,"

"Has he ride a lot?"

"Ya. Saw him riding last night after Birchwood did her walky. I donna think she was gotten make it back home, I was gonna ride her home but mum said no,"

Bettie only just realised that there was something amazing about young children. They always wanted to love, help and support others no matter what, if she was going to have kids, she had to teach them that. And then make sure they didn't lose it when they grew up.

"That's very good of you. Well done. Now where do I find this Jonny Boy?"

The kid shrugged, jumped on his bike and they both rode off again.

***

When Bettie returned to her little red car she was expecting to stare at her beautiful Graham bent over the engine failing to fix it. Instead she found the little old lady bend over and hammering away at the engine.

The wonderful smell of the warming Christmas spices filled the air as Bettie went up to Graham who had a few dark smudges on his white shirt and tight jeans, but he was still the sexy, most beautiful man Bettie had ever seen.

"At least you tried," Bettie said, rubbing

Graham's muscular shoulder.

"You clearly didn't trust me," Graham said, pretending to hit her cheek.

The little old lady climbed down to the ground and out of the car and turned to Bettie.

"Miss, your car should be working again in no time. Cars advanced a lot since the war but it will work,"

"You worked in the war?" Bettie asked, doubting the old lady was old enough to serve during World War Two.

"Oh no Miss, me dad served and I was born later. He taught me a lot about cars, trucks and planes from the war. I was quite the fixer in the neighbourhood. Have you found the Great Give Away?"

"The Great Give Away?" Graham asked.

Bettie just waved Graham silent.

"That's why I came to find you. One, thank you for your father's service. Two, who is Jonny Boy?"

The Little Old Lady shrugged.

"I met two kids who called him that and said he had a bike for big boys. Maybe he's an older kid or a young adult?" Bettie said.

"Oh! Miss, you mean Jonathan Bodie,"

Now Bettie shrugged. She didn't know anyone on the street, and yet this woman was acting like Bettie was a local.

"Um yes. Where is he?" Bettie asked.

The little old lady started to walk down the street.

"Come on Miss English. I'm waiting for a part from my garage. My Husband will find it soon. I'll show you where he lives,"

Bettie gestured Graham to follow and they both

followed the little old lady down the street. Even with the sun high in the sky, Bettie couldn't believe how cold and dark it was, but that was the strange thing about English weather, it never seemed natural.

The days were meant to get brighter after the Winter Solstice but they seemed to be getting darker and darker and darker, and even at ten O'clock it wasn't what Bettie would call bright.

But the strangeness of the English weather was something she loved about it though.

After a few more minutes of walking down the street, the little old lady pointed to a bright red and green door with a large wreath on it.

Bettie went up to it and knocked three times.

"Mr Bodie," Bettie said.

A tall man opened the door and Bettie was immediately taken by the amount of aftershave he was wearing, she had to focus on not passing out of its strength. It wasn't even a nice aftershave, not like the earthy, sexy one Graham was wearing.

"Merry Christmas!" Jonathan Bodie said in a happy manly voice.

"Um, Happy Christmas. Did you ride your bike last night?" Bettie asked.

She wanted to start off easy and at least place him at the scene of the crime before outright accusing him. Yet the man seemed too happy and filled with the Christmas spirit to want to steal and ruin the Christmas Season for others.

"Oh Yes, I love cycling. It's wonderful. Especially seeing all the amazing lights. Have you seen them! Have you seen them!"

Bettie nodded. "They are wonderful. Did you go to the Give Away... cage last night?"

Bodie's expression changed to a solid frown and his eyes flicked towards Graham.

Bettie clicked her fingers at him. "Yes he is a cop. But I'm not. Confess to me and nothing can happen to you. I won't tell him, you have my word,"

Bodie's eyes flicked between Bettie and Graham and a few times at the little old lady.

"The homeless peeps can't have the food. We need it. Well, my daughter's charity needs it,"

Bettie shook her head. "You're telling me. You stole the food for the good of others?"

Bodie's eyes widened and he frantically nodded.

Bettie looked at Graham and the little old lady.

"We're going to need a cup of tea for this one," she said.

"Bodie, let the Miss and Graham come in," the little old lady said.

Bettie looked at Bodie who slowly nodded his head and stepped out of the way.

***

The living room of Bodie's house was a lot nicer than Bettie had imagined. She loved his bright blue three seat sofa, chair opposite it and coffee table in the middle.

The living room was definitely small and minimalist but Bodie had managed to make it comforting and cozy and rather lovely despite its size.

There were a few pictures of his wife and presumably his three children on the walls and seeing all those pictures and the happiness of the family made Bettie just stare at Graham.

He was happy, sexy and beautiful, a perfect man who would make an amazing dad. Then she would make a great mother she supposed, Bettie loved her nephew Sean like her own child and had raised him (sometimes) a lot more than his own parents.

So maybe she could have children.

"Please sit down," Bodie said gesturing towards the three seat sofa as he sat down on the chair opposite them.

Bettie sat down. "Your daughter works for a charity?"

Bodie looked at the little old lady. "I'm sorry Margaret. I didn't mean to steal it. My daughter... my daughter just wanted a little help,"

"It's fine deary. But why didn't you just ask?"

Bodie looked to the ground. "I was embarrassed,"

"What is the charity?" Bettie asked.

"It's brilliant Miss. I love it. It's a new charity that helps the homeless, vulnerable youths and even the elderly,"

"My daughter wanted a little help. I didn't want the Great Give Away to only go to one type of person," Bodie said.

Bettie could agree with that. Her nephew could have been one of the vulnerable youths if her (idiot) of a brother-in-law had kicked him out when her nephew said he was gay. Sure Sean would have been homeless but he was still a vulnerable youth, it wasn't fair that he wouldn't necessarily benefit from the Great Give Away, just because he was young.

And most homeless in the area were older.

Bettie leant forward. "Graham I don't think there's a crime here if we reach an agreement,"

Graham smiled and Bettie loved that sexy movie star smile.

"Me either Bet, but what sort of agreement?"

Graham said.

"Well why don't you Mr Bodie and... Margaret agree to support your daughter's charity with the Great Give Away so she can help even more people?"

Both Bodie and Margaret looked at each other and smiled.

"Oh Miss that is a wonderful idea. That way we can all help the homeless, young and the elderly! That is marvellous!"

Bodie nodded too and judging by his face he was trying to hold back some tears.

Bettie stood up and looked at Bodie. "Just to check I presume the food is all in the garage safe and sound,"

Bodie nodded.

"Good. We will leave you both to sort out the details," Bettie said with a smile.

Graham started to head out the door and Bettie went to follow him when Margaret grabbed her arm.

"Thank you Miss! Thank you. You've saved the Great Give Away. What do I owe you?"

Judging by the look on Graham's face as he looked outside, her car was fixed and there was something wonderful about the little street.

Unlike the normal streets of southeast England, this one actually had soul, character and love in it. All these people no matter their background all loved each other in their own unique ways and wanted to help others. Hence the Great Give Away, Bettie wasn't going to charge people who wanted to help out others and help make the world a better place.

"Nothing," Bettie said smiling and walking out of the house. "Merry Great Give Away and A Happy New Year,"

Bettie heard Margaret and Bodie laugh, talk and being happy as she left, and her and Graham walked back up the street towards her car that was working perfectly.

There was a little old man walking away covered in oil and black smudges. He had to be Margaret's husband and the one who fixed the car properly.

She really wished everyone on the street, in England and the rest of the world had a great day and in some small way benefited from the Great Give Away. Because for some reason, a reason even Bettie didn't understand, she truly believed that every little act of kindness helped to make the world a better place.

Bettie wrapped her arm around Graham's waist and buried her face into his shoulder.

"When we get home tonight, we're so doing two things," Bettie said.

"What?"

"We're going to empty the house of the leftovers and take it down to the food bank,"

Graham smile and nodded at that.

Bettie stopped and pulled Graham close. "And we're going to make a baby,"

Graham's face lit up, they kissed and Bettie loved the soft feeling of his lips.

"Merry Great Give Away Bet,"

As Bettie pressed her lips against his, the entire world felt right as she had saved a made-up holiday for people, helped a charity and now she was going to be something she never thought she had wanted.

A mother.

And she had done that all before Eleven O'clock in the morning. A great, brilliant, perfect start to an amazing day.

GET YOUR FREE AND EXCLUSIVE SHORT STORY NOW! LEARN ABOUT NEMESIO'S PAST!

https://www.subscribepage.com/fireheart

About the author:

Connor Whiteley is the author of over 60 books in the sci-fi fantasy, nonfiction psychology and books for writer's genre and he is a Human Branding Speaker and Consultant.

He is a passionate warhammer 40,000 reader, psychology student and author.

Who narrates his own audiobooks and he hosts The Psychology World Podcast.

All whilst studying Psychology at the University of Kent, England.

Also, he was a former Explorer Scout where he gave a speech to the Maltese President in August 2018 and he attended Prince Charles' 70th Birthday Party at Buckingham Palace in May 2018.

Plus, he is a self-confessed coffee lover!

More From The Holiday Extravaganza:

<u>Criminal Christmas:</u>
Crime, Christmas, Closet
Protecting Christmas
Christmas Thief
Christmas, Crime, letter
Private Eye, Convention and Christmas
Cheater At Dinner
Perfect Christmas
Salvation In The Maid
Criminal, Resistance, Alliance
Dark Farm
Great Give Away

<u>Sweet Christmas</u>
Lights, Love, Christmas
Journalist, Zookeeper, Love
Young Romantic Hearts
Love In The Newspaper
Holiday, Burnout, Love
Homeless, Charity, Love
Cold December Night
Driving Home For Love
Love At The Winter Wedding
Fireworks, New Year, Love
Loving In The New Year Tourist

Fantastical Christmas:
Magic That Binds
One Final Christmas
Author's Christmas Problems
Last Winter Dragon Egg
A Sacrifice For Saturnalia
Soulcaster
Weird First Christmas
All Feast
Solstice Guardian
Wheel of Years
Repent

OTHER SHORT STORIES BY CONNOR WHITELEY

<u>Mystery Short Stories:</u>
Poison In The Candy Cane
Christmas Innocence
You Better Watch Out
Christmas Theft
Trouble In Christmas
Smell of The Lake
Problem In A Car
Theft, Past and Team
Embezzler In The Room
A Strange Way To Go
A Horrible Way To Go
Ann Awful Way To Go
An Old Way To Go
A Fishy Way To Go
A Pointy Way To Go
A High Way To Go
A Fiery Way To Go
A Glassy Way To Go
A Chocolatey Way To Go
Kendra Detective Mystery Collection Volume 1
Kendra Detective Mystery Collection Volume 2
Stealing A Chance At Freedom

Glassblowing and Death
Theft of Independence
Cookie Thief
Marble Thief
Book Thief
Art Thief
Mated At The Morgue
The Big Five Whoopee Moments
Stealing An Election
Mystery Short Story Collection Volume 1
Mystery Short Story Collection Volume 2

Science Fiction Short Stories:
The First Rememberer
Life of A Rememberer
System of Wonder
Lifesaver
Remarkable Way She Died
The Interrogation of Annabella Stormic
Blade of The Emperor
Arbiter's Truth
Computation of Battle
Old One's Wrath
Puppets and Masters
Ship of Plague
Interrogation
Edge of Failure

One Way Choice
Acceptable Losses
Balance of Power
Good Idea At The Time
Escape Plan
Escape In The Hesitation
Inspiration In Need
Singing Warriors
Knowledge is Power
Killer of Polluters
Climate of Death
The Family Mailing Affair
Defining Criminality
The Martian Affair
A Cheating Affair
The Little Café Affair
Mountain of Death
Prisoner's Fight
Claws of Death
Bitter Air
Honey Hunt
Blade On A Train

<u>Fantasy Short Stories:</u>
City of Snow
City of Light
City of Vengeance

Dragons, Goats and Kingdom
Smog The Pathetic Dragon
Don't Go In The Shed
The Tomato Saver
The Remarkable Way She Died
The Bloodied Rose
Asmodia's Wrath
Heart of A Killer
Emissary of Blood
Dragon Coins
Dragon Tea
Dragon Rider
Sacrifice of the Soul
Heart of The Flesheater
Heart of The Regent
Heart of The Standing
Feline of The Lost
Heart of The Story
City of Fire
Awaiting Death

Other books by Connor Whiteley:

Bettie English Private Eye Series
A Very Private Woman
The Russian Case
A Very Urgent Matter
A Case Most Personal
Trains, Scots and Private Eyes
The Federation Protects

The Fireheart Fantasy Series
Heart of Fire
Heart of Lies
Heart of Prophecy
Heart of Bones
Heart of Fate

City of Assassins (Urban Fantasy)
City of Death
City of Marytrs
City of Pleasure
City of Power

Agents of The Emperor
Return of The Ancient Ones
Vigilance
Angels of Fire
Kingmaker

The Garro Series- Fantasy/Sci-fi
GARRO: GALAXY'S END
GARRO: RISE OF THE ORDER
GARRO: END TIMES
GARRO: SHORT STORIES
GARRO: COLLECTION
GARRO: HERESY
GARRO: FAITHLESS
GARRO: DESTROYER OF WORLDS
GARRO: COLLECTIONS BOOK 4-6
GARRO: MISTRESS OF BLOOD
GARRO: BEACON OF HOPE
GARRO: END OF DAYS

Winter Series- Fantasy Trilogy Books
WINTER'S COMING
WINTER'S HUNT
WINTER'S REVENGE
WINTER'S DISSENSION

Miscellaneous:
RETURN
FREEDOM
SALVATION
Reflection of Mount Flame
The Masked One
The Great Deer

www.ingramcontent.com/pod-product-compliance
Lightning Source LLC
LaVergne TN
LVHW011851060526
838200LV00054B/4278